Fraser!

Not Way Too TALL After All!

Written by Joy M. O'Hora©
Illustrated by Mairead Brennan

To Claire,
who loved children.

About **1,000 sleeps ago**, Fraser, a tall fir tree, stood in a small pretty forest, on the edge of a busy town.

Every December, as soon as school finished for the Holidays, townspeople visited. They wanted to choose a fir tree as their Christmas or Holiday tree.

Peoples of all ages, families of all shapes and sizes, big and small, travelled to the forest!

Some families had brothers and sisters, some had a Mom or Dad, some had both. Some kids arrived with their Gran or Grandad and some had two Dads and two Moms.

On days the families arrived, the pretty forest was filled with laughter, colour and excitement! Fraser's branches shook in anticipation, he waited to be chosen.

Fraser waited... patiently.

Fraser knew about the Holidays and Christmas from nature walks the junior school children took with their teachers.

As the long line of kids wound their way around the forest, their teachers explained how some of the trees would, someday, be Christmas trees and that it could take 10 years or more for the littlest trees to grow.

The teachers described how the trees would be all lit up with twinkly lights, and best of all, crowned with a big star on the very tippy-top branch.

Oh, how Fraser longed to be picked.

Holiday Season after Holiday Season, kids would run excitedly up to him, shouting back at the adults, "THIS ONE! *Pick this one! Its branches go WAY way way up high!*" but the adults always chuckled, shook their heads kindly and declared Fraser to be "*Way Too Tall!*"

Sometimes, the littlest kids hugged Fraser and...
well... that made Fraser feel better.

The seasons passed. Big winds whooshed, snows swirled, all around the forest, then settled softly. Rain pelted down, softening the earth, the sun warmed and brightened everything in the forest.

Fraser stood on... he waited, patiently, still, deeply rooted to his mother earth... friends with all the birds and flowers of the forest.

As the seasons changed, Fraser kept growing, his branches stretching right-up to the clouds or clear blue sky by day and the navy black star-filled sky by night. Fraser dreamed about reaching those stars and wearing a star on his top branch.

Fraser was now the tallest tree in the forest for miles and miles! Fraser felt so alive, so fresh, breathing out his pure pine-scented air for every living creature, plant and townspeople to enjoy.

More Holiday Seasons came and went and went again.

Fraser stood on patiently, waiting, watching all the other trees in the forest getting picked.

Do you know...
Sometimes, when we are patient and grateful, just standing still, change happens all by itself... without any fuss or bother.

And... one wintry afternoon Fraser got a huge surprise. Just as dusk was settling for yet another day, a group of people dressed in bright yellow overalls, arrived in a **ginormous, long red truck**. They wore black heavy boots. They looked serious.

They immediately spotted Fraser - the tallest tree in the forest. They surrounded him...

Fraser had been chosen!!

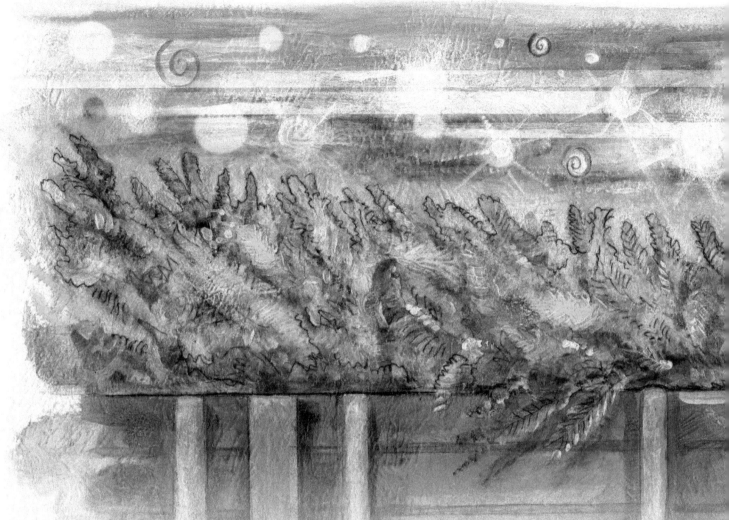

Fraser's branches swelled with pride, he took a big deep
breath as the yellow-overall people took out their saws
and cut him away from his mother earth.
It did not hurt.

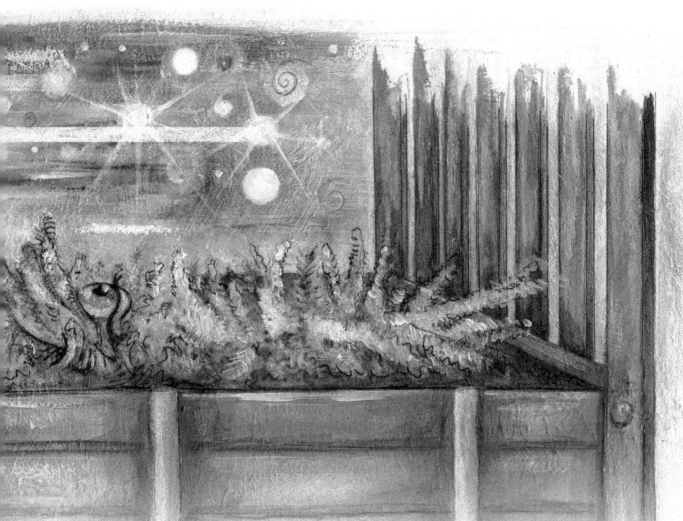

After much huffing, puffing, hefting and hollering, Fraser found himself laying down in the back of that **long ginormous truck**. The navy black night sky streaked with yellow lights, raced by.

After a snooze Fraser was hoisted to a standing position again, his roots no longer planted in mother earth but plunged into a bucket of ice-cold water. It was refreshing.

Fraser wondered where he was. This home was nothing like the homes described by the teachers on nature walks...

Fraser wondered when the one big star he longed
for, would appear for him to wear...

Fraser's new home, was, in fact, the large entrance hall of a block of offices downtown.

The building had very high ceilings...

It was perfect, just perfect for him.

All day long people dressed in suits dashed by Fraser, speaking on, or gazing at phones, dazed, and distracted, everyone lost in their own world.

At night, the building was empty of dashing-by people, except for Don, the Security Guard, who sat in a little cubicle near Fraser. Don read his newspaper or scrolled, bored, looking at his phone! Occasionally, Don had a little sleep, with his head resting on his newspaper, the pages fluttered softly up and down as he snored gently at his desk.

Again, Fraser stood patiently, waiting. Fraser felt pleased... a couple of sleeps later his patience and gratitude were rewarded...

Bright and early, two ladies - one short, one tall, who normally dashed by, arrived carrying a big sign.
They placed the sign right next to Fraser...

The sign read:

"Help our Junior School, Buy a Little Star, Decorate our Tree!"

And do you know... the other dashing-by people did just that... after all, it was the Holidays!

Soon, Fraser, whose top branch almost touched the ceiling of the tall building (but not quite) was all dressed. Each branch covered with small bright, helpful stars shining, twinkling, winking.

Fraser beamed, he was a golden shimmering light of powerful patience. Fraser was majestic!

And something else happened...
All, absolutely ALL of the dashing-by people stopped, they stood, still. They put down their phones and stood, just like Fraser in the forest. They stared up at him in awe and gratitude.

The dashing-by people used their phones to take photos of themselves and their friends with Fraser, oh how they all laughed! It was the jolliest of times.

Best of all, the school kids came to visit. They sang songs, and the dashing-by people joined in. The kids were rewarded with hot chocolate and red and white candy canes.

Then, the smallest child with the help of Don, climbed the big sturdy ladder and placed the star, that Fraser had so wanted, on his tippy-top branch.

Everyone clapped and cheered, then sighed and declared Fraser to be the best tree ever!

Fraser smiled to himself. The children and the dashing-by people could not *see* his smile, they could *feel* his smile and they smiled too and at each other.

Fraser was **Not Way Too TALL After All!**

The days passed, the dashing-by people left to go home for the holidays. Fraser was becoming sleepier with each passing day. When Don finally locked up the building for the holidays, as he tipped his cap at Fraser to say goodbye, Fraser was finding it hard to breathe.

Uprooted from his forest earth, with just the warm air of the building, Fraser's energy was slowly, but surely slipping away.

After a few more sleeps, Fraser's top branch, that one that almost touched the ceiling, but not quite, dipped over. The big, beautiful star that held on his tippy top branch, tumbled to the cold shiny floor below, it bounced and rolled just a little, then came to a stop, unbroken.

Fraser then went to sleep forever.

His job was done...

When the Holiday Season ended, those same people in bright yellow overalls came and laid Fraser in that same ginormous truck. They brought Fraser back to his forest!

There, along with all the other now fast asleep forever Holiday trees, Fraser was recycled, and all his goodness, patience and majesty were sprinkled far and wide, right back on his mother earth, to nourish and grow more trees.

So... no matter what kind of tall or small you are, every tall or small is here for a special reason. There is a place for everyone, all sizes, in this world of ours.

Reach for your star... the world is perfect for you, and you are perfect for this world!

The End... *until a new fir tree grows,*
maybe as tall as Fraser... or smaller... maybe.